Seven Clues
in Pebble Creek

A LORIMER BLUE KITE MYSTERY

Seven Clues in Pebble Creek

Kathy Stinson

James Lorimer & Company, Publishers
Toronto, 1987

1-55028-036-8 paper   1-55028-038-4 cloth

Cover Design: Dreadnaught
Illustrations: Don Besco

Canadian Cataloguing in Publication Data

Stinson, Kathy.
  Seven clues in Pebble Creek

(A Lorimer blue kite mystery)
ISBN 1-55028-038-4 (bound).   ISBN 1-55028-036-8
(pbk.)

I. Title.   II. Series.

PS8587.I56Se8 1987   jC813'.54   C87-094480-0
PZ7.S74Se 1987

James Lorimer & Company, Publishers,
Egerton Ryerson Memorial Building,
35 Britain St.,
Toronto, M5A 1R7

To my mom who led me to my love of words and books...

1

It was only a week into the summer holiday, and already Matt was bored. Slouched against the front porch railing, he socked his baseball into his mitt again and again. He was bored with Happy Days reruns on TV. Bored with the same old pile of comics. Bored with the sound of the baseball slapping into his glove. Bored with being bored. He was so bored, he was even thinking about cleaning his room, just for something to do.

Matt sighed a bored sigh. He chucked his ball and mitt into the corner of the porch. He picked his battered bike up from the brown grass in front of his house. Then he straightened the crooked seat and hopped on before the seat could slip out of place again.

Passing the empty house next door, Matt kicked the "Sold" sign on its lawn. How many hours had he spent in there on Tim's computer, in dungeons and haunted forests, in mazes and at race tracks? It didn't matter. Now Tim was gone.

Everybody was gone — even his best friend, Mike Lennox, who was *always* there.

Turning onto the paved path that ran through the shady ravine to Bricker Street, Matt heard a horrible grinding sound under him.

"Fritters," he cursed. He stopped and hooked his drooping bike chain back where it belonged. Then he headed off.

Farther into the ravine, he turned right onto a narrow dirt path. His bike rattled over a bumpy section, until the path took a sudden dip down and back up. At the top of the dip, Matt turned sharply to the right. The path became very narrow and the ferns and weeds caught at his feet. He braked just short of a boulder barely visible among the dense undergrowth and let his bike fall into the bushes at the side of the path. Then he pushed through them and slid down the curved bank to the side of the creek.

This was Matt's favourite spot. Nobody knew about it but him. He came here whenever he had some thinking to do, or when he just wanted to be alone.

Matt wiggled in the cool sand of the bank. Splashes of sunlight danced on the ground and sparkled on the water. His body soon formed a comfortable hollow in the sand.

He picked up a pebble from the side of the creek and hurled it. He counted the number of times it skipped across the water. Six. He picked up another and tried again. Four.

Matt sighed. Tim was lucky moving into the city. There was nothing to do in a small town like Pebble Creek. Matt pitched another pebble across the creek. It glubbed to the bottom after one skip. Then he turned to climb back up the bank to his bike. It was no fun being alone when you had to be.

Matt dragged his bike from the bushes and started back out. Close to the main path, he stopped suddenly and ducked behind the bushes. Shuffling along the paved path was the one person he did not want to run into, no matter how bored and lonely he was. Mr. Grubb.

Mr. Grubb lived in the big dark house at the end of Booth Street. He was so huge that the grey trousers bagging around his long skinny legs stopped far above his sagging grey socks and grey slippers. The sleeves of his grey sweater, which he wore no matter what the weather, came nowhere near his wrists.

Everything about Mr. Grubb seemed to be grey, from his shaggy hair tucked behind his large ears, to his bushy eye-

brows and piercing eyes. His jowly cheeks pulled his mouth down in a grey frown that never went away. The bony hand that clutched his heavy wooden cane was grey. Even his raspy voice sounded grey. The old man was so colourless that Matt sometimes wondered if he might be a ghost.

Matt pulled himself more tightly into the bushes. He didn't actually believe in ghosts. Not really. But strange things happened at the big old house at the end of Booth Street.

When he was sure Mr. Grubb was well gone, Matt ventured out and turned along the path toward Bricker Street. Outside the Bricker Variety Store, he parked his bike in the bike-rack. The bell jingled as he pushed open the screen door.

"Hi, Matt," greeted Martha. "What's it going to be today? Milk? Newspaper? Jujubes?"

"Jujubes are boring. I just came in to say hi."

"Jujubes boring?" Martha shoved her wire-framed glasses up her nose. "Matt Randall, you love jujubes. What's wrong?"

"There's nobody around," complained Matt. "Mike's gone to his cousin's. John and Tony are camping with their dad.

There's nothing to do when there's nobody to do it with." He flipped through the rack of comics, but there were none he hadn't already read at least six times. He sighed and dragged his feet back to the door.

"Don't look so glum, chum," chirped Martha. "Something will turn up, you'll see."

"Yeah, sure." The bell jingled as he left.

He pulled into his driveway just as Eleanor started up his front walk with her bag of mail.

"Matt Randall?" she said.

Matt looked up in surprise. "That's me."

"Postcard."

"For me?"

"If you're Matt Randall of Number Three Booth Street."

"Yeah. Thanks." Matt looked to see which of his vacationing friends had thought to send him a postcard. It said:

There's something you should look
For. It will bring you great
Pleasure.
Not coins in a pirate's chest, but
A different sort of treasure.
Be clever, be brave, and you'll
Get to the end.
Along the way, you might need
A friend.
The treasure's got old parts,
But new ones, too.
Go to the right bus stop now.
You'll find another clue.

There was no signature.

Matt stared at the message. Go to the right bus stop. A different sort of treasure. Was this like a treasure hunt? Why him? Matt's head was spinning.

Eleanor dropped the rest of the mail into the Randalls' mailbox. Then she winked at Matt and continued on her route, whistling.

Matt examined the postcard again. On the front was a picture of a windmill and a girl wearing wooden shoes and holding tulips. A postcard from Holland? But it didn't have a foreign postage stamp. Studying the faint postmark, Matt barely made out the word, Mazurk. Mazurk was a town not far from Pebble Creek.

Could somebody have bought the postcard in Holland and not sent it till they got home to Mazurk? Maybe, but he knew no one who had been to Holland, or who lived in Mazurk.

"Mom," Matt called, going inside. "Mom, do we know anybody...?"

His mother had the telephone tucked between her ear and her shoulder. Bills and bank statements were spread out on the table in front of her. She waved Matt away crossly. Matt shrugged. Re-reading the message, he wandered back outside.

"You might need a friend," the card said. Terrific. Where was he supposed to find a friend?

Matt looked longingly at the houses across the street and between them to the empty baseball field. There was no one for baseball and there was no one for a treasure hunt.

So what, he decided. The note just said he *might* need a friend. It also said that at the right bus stop he would find another clue. He jammed the postcard into his pocket and straightened the seat of his bike.

A few minutes later his bike clattered to the ground beside Bricker Variety. He pushed open the screen door.

"Martha, what do you think about..." but Martha was not alone. Leaning on the counter across from her was a person with pink hair, green lips, and jagged lines painted around her eyes.

"You again?" asked Martha. "What's new?"

The other girl stared down at him. Matt felt very small. "Just..." He couldn't ask Martha about the postcard now. "Nothing."

"Oh, Martha," drawled the husky

voice of Martha's friend, "he's cute."

Matt darted for the door. He let it slam behind him. He was leaning against the side of the building, feeling stupid, when he spotted something unusual. Quite low on the wooden bus-stop post in front of the Bricker Variety was a piece of paper.

Maybe it was a scrap blown against the post by the wind. Matt stepped a bit closer. The paper had been folded and tacked to the post.

Matt pulled the paper free and tucked it into his pocket. He grabbed his bike. The paper made a comfortable lump in his pocket. He turned onto the path leading to his place by the river. Bump, rattle rattle, dip down, dip up, sharp turn right, narrow narrow, boulder, through the bushes, and down the bank.

So what if he couldn't figure out who was behind the search, or what he was looking for, or why he might need a friend to help find it. He had found the second clue, and it was the clues that were going to lead him to the treasure.

His hands shaking, Matt pulled the lump of paper from his pocket and unfolded it.

2

The paper was blank. Blank on both sides. "Fritters."

Matt looked at his postcard again. "Be clever," it said. He should have known that counted him out. His brains never had been his strong point. He dug a hole in the sand with the heel of his shoe. If he was too stupid to find one clue, how did he think he could ever find a treasure?

Matt buried the blank paper in the hole he had dug. Then he climbed back up the bank of the river and got back on his bike. Riding around town, he wished he had never seen the mysterious postcard. Now he felt bored and lonely, and stupid.

Passing the gas station, Matt noticed another bus stop with another piece of paper tacked to it. He rode past. This looked like someone's idea of a joke. And he wasn't going to be made to look like a fool.

But what if there really was another clue? Was it stupid to go on looking? Or stupid to give up already?

Wheeling past the library, Matt saw that there was a scrap of paper tacked to this bus stop, too. A group of teenagers lay in the grass waiting for the bus.

Pedalling slowly, he wished Mike Lennox were here. He'd know what to do.

Matt circled back. It wouldn't hurt just to check. He yanked the paper free and tucked it into his pocket. He straightened the seat on his bike and pulled away. A wave of laughter spread through the gang on the grass.

Matt's face reddened. So it *was* a joke. His hopes for a summer adventure were dashed by the laughing voices behind him. Pedalling fast along Bricker Street, he tried to tell himself it didn't matter. He hadn't really believed in the treasure hunt. If he hadn't been so bored, he wouldn't have paid any attention at all to the stupid postcard. So, he was just back to being bored Matt Randall looking forward to a boring summer. So what.

Matt pulled up beside a garbage basket outside the post office. Before throwing in the paper he had taken from the bus stop by the library, he opened it.

There was scrunched-up printing on it, just like the scrunched-up printing on the postcard. His heart pounding, he sat down on the curb.

Eleanor trudged up beside the post office with her empty mailbag. "How's the detective business?" she asked.

Matt shrugged and shook his head. Eleanor winked. When she had gone inside, Matt read:

To find the next clue, you must go
Where books are lined up row on row.
Six shelves in on the right hand side
Look in the back of a book very wide.
Be sure no one sees you near this
Spot
And with these clues do not get
Caught.

A cold shiver tickled up Matt's spine.
But he knew what he had to do.

Matt beetled back to the library. He
strode up the broad steps into the old
stone building. In the cool, quiet room,
two high-school students were thumbing
through the magazines. The children's
librarian was helping a father choose some
books for his youngster. Otherwise the
library seemed to be empty.

Matt counted off the shelves on the
right-hand side, feeling very out of place
in the middle of the adult section. When
he reached the sixth shelf, he gave a
hurried look across all the books for one

that was very wide. They all looked wider than anything he had ever read.

He pulled out a blue book that looked especially thick, but inside the back cover he found nothing. He checked a few other big ones, but no luck.

Then, on a shelf high above him, Matt saw a thick grey book, definitely thicker than any other book on the shelf. He pulled a nearby footstool over to the shelf, but even at a full stretch, he could not reach it.

This must be where the friend comes in, Matt thought. Fritters. As he stepped down from the stool, a movement behind the books froze him in his tracks. Some-one was looking at the books on the other side of the sixth shelf. No, not at the books, Matt realized, but at him!

There was something familiar about the jagged lines around the eyes that were staring through the books at him. Matt remembered. *"Oh, Martha, he's cute."*

In a gruff whisper the green lips

behind the books hissed, "I know what you're after." When the creature began to slink around to his side of the shelf, Matt ran.

He scrambled down the steps, grabbed his bike and pedalled hard through the ravine. Sweat trickled down his face and soaked the back of his shirt. Matt steered his bike along one of the side paths that led to a wooden bridge over the creek.

Panting, he dropped his bike on the bridge and plunked himself down on the wooden planks. He yanked off his sneakers and socks. As his feet dangled in the cool water, his racing heart returned to its normal pace.

What did Martha's weird friend want with him? In spite of the sun warming his back, Matt shivered.

He jumped when the boards thump-bumped behind him. Approaching on a brand-new red BMX bicycle was David Varvarikos.

Matt stared for a moment. Could that really be David? Matt didn't think he'd ever seen David on a bike. At school when his work was done, which was almost always, David never goofed off or shot spitballs. He stayed at his desk, reading. Even at recess he stood by the wall of the school with his nose in a book. And he walked home that way, too. He never played sports. The one time Ms. Symon made David play baseball in gym, he didn't even know how to hold the bat. Matt figured David didn't know how to do anything, except read.

David dismounted, leaned his bike against the rail on the bridge, and sat down beside Matt.

Matt tried not to look at the shiny bicycle leaning on the rail. He tried not to look at David sitting with his arms looped through the other rail.

"That your bike?" Matt finally asked David.

"Yup."

Matt looked at the clean black tires and the shiny chrome handlebars.

"Looks brand new," he observed.

"Yup."

"I didn't think you knew how to ride a bike."

"I know how. I just never had one of my own before."

Fritters. David already thought he was too smart. With this bike, David would be a royal pain.

"My parents gave it to me for passing with honours," David boasted.

"You're kidding," laughed Matt. "You couldn't not pass with honours if you tried."

"I know. But it's a good excuse for a present just the same."

"I'll have to try that one on my parents. I never got anything for passing." Matt turned the idea over in his mind. "I wonder if I could talk them into buying me a computer."

"Hardly," choked David. "A computer costs a lot more than a bike, and if your parents can't even afford to buy you a decent bike, well..." David pulled a paperback book from his shorts and started to read.

Matt stared at David. His straight black hair hung neatly. His white shirt was tucked neatly into his crisply ironed shorts. His nose was neatly buried in his book. Matt felt like dumping neat David into the river. But that was too obvious. He had a better idea.

3

"Wanna go riding?" challenged Matt.

"Okay."

David continued to read while Matt pulled his feet out of the water and dried them with his socks, which he then tied to his handlebars. He shoved his feet into his tattered sneakers and stood with his old blue bike.

"You coming?"

"Oh." David looked up. "I was waiting for you." He tucked his book into the back of his waistband and pulled up his socks.

"Ready?" Matt straightened his seat, hopped on his bike, and set off in the direction of the quarry and Stony Road.

"Ready." David mounted his bike and followed.

I bet you're not ready, thought Matt, for what I've got in mind.

The wheels of the old blue CCM and the new red BMX spun freely along the pavement. The breeze blew through the boys' hair and cooled their faces and necks. They had not gone far when Matt's bicycle ground to a stop. "Not now," he groaned. He kneeled to re-attach the chain.

"I'd better lead," crowed David.

"Frittering fudgsicles," Matt muttered, as the blur of red flashed past him. How dare that little...!

Matt put on a burst of speed to catch up. Above the north wall of the quarry, he pedalled casually past David.

"Hey," hollered David, but before he could pass, Matt veered left, his tires thunking off the main path to a dirt path below. David followed.

Now we'll see how smart you are, thought Matt. He led David on a meandering route among clumps of clay and rock to the quarry floor far below. He bumped over large stones and made sudden turns at odd angles to avoid holes and clumps of boulder. Where he was leading David wasn't really a path at all, and he expected at any moment to hear David's BMX cracking up behind him.

The two boys stood, both bicycles still intact, on the quarry floor. Matt shaded his eyes and gazed up the steep quarry walls at the zig-zagging route they had taken.

"I thought you were only good at reading," he huffed.

David beamed. "Did I surprise you?"

"Yeah." David might be a pain, but Matt had to admit that he could ride a bike. Matt himself had wondered if he was going to make it down in one or two spots. "That was a pretty rough piece of riding."

"Are you kidding? It was nothing."

"Oh, yeah?" Matt pointed to the section of quarry wall beside the route they had taken. It was a sheer cliff of smooth sand. "Then I guess you could ride down there easy, too, eh?"

David looked up. His fists twisted tightly around his handlegrips. "Sure."

"Okay, let's go." Together Matt and David dragged their bikes back up through the rocks and bushes, and over to the top of the wall of sand.

"Okay?" said David.

"On the count of three," dared Matt.

Together they counted. "One. Two. Three."

In disbelief, Matt saw David start down the steep slope. The sand gripped the front wheel of the BMX. Matt watched in horror as David flipped over the shining handlebars and rolled and rolled. David's arms kept reaching out as he tumbled, but there was nothing for his hands to grasp.

"David!" Matt screamed, sliding down the sand on his back. He couldn't believe David had tried it. For sure, Mike would never fall for a dare like that.

When finally David stopped tumbling, his body lay still on the hard floor of the quarry far below.

"I'm coming, David," Matt croaked. It was difficult to hurry when he had to be careful to keep leaning back, so he wouldn't pitch forward down the sand, too.

When Matt finally reached the bottom, David's clothes were twisted around his body. His hair was full of sand and sticking to his sweaty face. His cheeks were flushed, but his chest rose and fell with his breathing.

David groaned and tried to open his eyes. Matt shielded David's face from the bright sun. David sat up slowly.

"David, I thought you were supposed to be smart."

David shook the sand out of his shirt and tucked it back into his shorts. "My book," he wailed. "I lost my book."

"Forget the book! You could've killed yourself. What were you trying to prove?"

David picked up a handful of sand and watched it sift through his fingers. "I know what everybody says about me. You think just because I don't say much at school, and go to Greek school on Saturdays, I'm just a wimp."

Matt looked down and emptied the sand out of one of his shoes.

"I was afraid if I didn't ride down there with you, you'd keep thinking that," David finished.

"So you'd rather I thought you were a jerk?" asked Matt.

David shrugged.

Matt wandered over to a pile of rocks near where David had landed. He picked one up and hurled it at the "No Dumping" sign. It clanged when it hit. Matt reached for another rock. *Clang.* David was on his feet. He started hitting the target, too.

"Guess you're okay, eh?"

David hurled another rock and missed. *Thud.* "I'm okay."

Matt looked at him for a few moments. Then he took a deep breath. "Listen, there's ... well, something I have to get at the library. I could kind of use ... like ... a hand."

"What is it?"

"There's this book."

"What's it called? Maybe I have it." *Clang.*

"I forget. It's a thick grey book."

"How come you want to get a book

28

when you don't even know what the title is?"

"It's not really the book I want." Why did David have to ask so many questions? *Clang.*

"If it's not the book, what do you want?"

"There's this paper," explained Matt hesitantly, "that...um...my mom thinks she left in this book, only I don't think I can reach it." *Thud.*

"Why doesn't your mom get it herself?"

"Listen, I just need you to give me a boost so I can get this paper out of this book. Will you do that or not?"

"Okay," snapped David. "I'll help you get your stupid paper."

"Now?"

"Okay." And without another word, the boys went to fetch their bikes.

Later, on the stairs of the library, Matt paused. "There's a couple of things I should tell you before we go in."

"What?"

"Well, for one thing," Matt began, "we've got to make sure nobody sees us."

"Why?"

"We just do. And, don't wander around. Just follow me in, then out. Okay?"

"I guess so," said David. "But I'd sure like to know who made you boss."

"Look, it's my clue, isn't it?"

As soon as the words were out of his mouth, Matt realized his blunder.

4

"Clue?" pressed David. "What clue?"

Matt kicked a pebble down the library steps to the road. How could he get David to help now, without giving away everything?

"And don't try and cook up some story about your mother leaving a note in her big grey library book," warned David. "I'm not helping you until you tell me the truth."

Matt walked slowly down the steps and sat down under the huge maple in front of the library. David followed. Matt pulled the crumpled bus-stop note from his pocket, and the postcard.

Just then, Martha walked by. "Hey, Martha," called Matt. "I thought you were working."

"Somebody's covering for me." Martha pushed her glasses up her nose. "I just had to bring back this book of poetry. It's way overdue."

"You read poetry?" asked David. "Me, too."

"I read lots of poetry,' said Martha, pushing a wisp of hair behind her ear. "I like to write it, too."

"Martha!" gushed a husky voice. Down the steps of the library pranced Martha's weird friend.

"See you later, guys."

Martha's plain brown ponytail swung from side to side as she ran to meet her friend. Matt wondered how she and that pink-haired weirdo had ever started hanging around together.

David grabbed the postcard from Matt and read it. "Do you know who sent this?" he asked.

"No."

David stared at the card in his hand.

"Then I can't believe you're actually going to do what this card says."

"Why not? It says I'll find a treasure."

"Can't you tell when somebody's pulling your leg?" David flicked the clues to the ground.

Matt blushed. "But what about the clue at the bus stop?"

"So what?" jeered David. "I still say there's no treasure."

"You don't know everything," Matt hissed at David. "And what do you care if there's a treasure or not? I only asked you to help me get the book down. I didn't ask you to do the whole thing with me."

"Wait a second. This 'be sure no one sees you' and 'don't get caught' stuff means this could be dangerous. If I'm going to help you do anything, then I'm in on the treasure, too."

"*You* wait a second!" said Matt, now

standing above David. "One minute you say there is no treasure. The next minute, you're claiming your share!" He stomped off to get his bike from the rack. "Forget it. I'll find somebody else to get the book for me."

"Hey, wait. I'll do it."

"No."

"If you let me do it," pleaded David, "I'll let you ride my BMX."

Matt paused. His hands held the bare handlebars of his scruffy bike. The seat was torn and hung crookedly by one rusty piece of metal. Several spokes were missing. In the rack beside him was the gleaming red BMX, with black padded handlegrips, seat cover to match, and red-rimmed mag wheels.

Matt pretended to think it over for a minute. There really was no one else to help him.

"Okay."

The library was full of people. Nobody even noticed the two boys heading toward the adult section. When they reached the sixth shelf, Matt looked up with dread. What if someone else had taken the grey book? What if that creepy girl with the pink hair had it?

The book was still there. David made a cradle with his hands. Matt placed one foot in David's hands and pulled the book down from the shelf.

"Ouch!" yelped David. "My fingers!" Matt fell to the floor with a thud. "Ow!" Suddenly the library was quiet.

Quickly Matt found the slip of paper inside the back cover and shoved the book onto a lower shelf. Then, as he picked himself up from the floor, he found himself face to armpit with the librarian.

"What," squawked the librarian, "are you doing in this section of the library? The children's books are over there." She pointed, like the scarecrow in *The Wizard of Oz*.

Matt swallowed.

"I had to get a note that was left in the back of a book my mom had out," said David.

"And did you find it?"

"Yes. Thank you."

"Then I think perhaps you should get going, don't you?"

"Yes, ma'am," David said. "That is what we were just going to do."

Under the tree in front of the library Matt and David collapsed in a fit of giggles.

Matt kept a straight face long enough to mimic David, "That is what we were just going to do," then burst into giggles again. David hugged his aching sides, laughing, too.

"And what was that about a note your mother left in a book?" squealed Matt.

"It came in handy, that dumb story."

Matt jumped on David. David rolled Matt onto his back and began tickling him. "So, let's see the note."

"No," Matt squeaked, trying to catch his breath.

"Come on," begged David, "after that close call and *my* clean getaway?"

Finally Matt escaped. He grabbed David's bike from the rack. "You owe me a ride on your bike."

Matt thrilled to the feel of David's new BMX beneath him, as David cycled along on Matt's creaky CCM. Riding into the wooded ravine, David said suddenly, "I think I know who sent you the postcard."

"Who?"

"A very bad poet," said David.

"Yeah. A bad Dutch poet," added Matt. He eyed David skeptically. "Since when do you know any Dutch poets?" Why did David always have to make sure everyone knew that he knew more than anybody else?

"Ages," David said. "You do, too."

"I do?" Matt looked at David blankly. "Who?"

David laughed.

Matt braked to a sudden stop. "Quit acting so superior. I already know you're smarter than me. Just tell me."

"If I do," bargained David, "I want in on the rest of the treasure hunt."

"No," snapped Matt. He dropped David's bike to the ground.

"Easy," yelled David. "That's a valuable vehicle you're handling."

"*So--orry.*" He grabbed his own bike from David, straightened its seat, and pedalled away.

"Don't you want to know who the mystery poet is?" called David.

Matt paused for a moment. Then he pulled away furiously. He didn't stop until he had reached the wooden bridge. He pulled the paper from his pocket and unfolded it. David rode up behind him.

"Okay, who?" mumbled Matt.

"I do the treasure hunt with you?"

"Yeah, yeah."

"Scout's honour?"

"Scout's honour."

"Cross your heart?"

"Cross my heart."

"Spit on a rock?"

"David," Matt groaned, "just tell me who sent the postcard. Before I change my mind."

5

"The mystery poet," David announced, "is Martha."

"She's Dutch?"

"What kind of name do you think Van Loon is? Pig Latin?"

"But, if it's Martha, well...how can it be a real treasure hunt? It's more like some stupid game. And I'm not playing."

"Come on, Matt. Even if it is just a game, do we really have anything better to do?"

Matt shrugged. "I guess not."

Matt held the paper flat. Together the boys read:

Rocks and not paper are found in
A quarry
Except for today, and your only worry

Is under which rocks for the clues
Must you look?
By the North wall? By the brook?
The treasure has big parts and
Little parts, too.
It's okay for one, even better for
Two.

"Not the quarry," complained Matt.
"It's so hot down there."

"We could go get an ice cream first."

Inside the Pebble Creek Ice Cream
Store, David held a place in the long line
while Matt hung around the Space Demons video game in the corner of the store.
The space demons demolished the last
space ship, and the tall girl playing walked
away laughing. Matt stepped forward. It
was his turn. Space Demons had been one
of his best games on Tim's computer. He
dropped his quarter into the slot, ready
for action. Immediately a burly teenager
elbowed him away.

"Fritters," Matt muttered.

"Whadyusay?"

"Nothing." He joined David in line.

Afterwards on the bench in front of the store, Matt licked a chocolatey drip running down the side of his cone. "I'm trying to eat my way through all the flavours of ice cream before the end of the summer," he said.

"So am I," said David. "How many have you had so far?"

"How many have you?"

"I asked you first."

"Five, I think," muttered Matt.

"Oh. I've just had three."

"Me, too," Matt admitted.

"Turkey." David laughed.

Matt grinned. "You know what would be a good treasure?"

"What?"

"Gift certificates for a summer's worth of ice cream cones."

David crunched into the edge of his cone. "I think it will be something even better than that."

"Like what?"

"I'd be happy if it was money," said David, "a tremendous pile of money."

Matt nodded. "I heard of a guy who found a suitcase full of money in a ditch once. He turned it over to the police, but nobody claimed it, so he got to keep it." He looked over the clue again. "But what we're looking for isn't money."

"How do you know?"

"Money's small, for one thing. The note says big parts and little parts."

"Maybe those are big bills like hundreds and little bills like ones."

"The note also said the treasure would be better for two. Who wants to share money?"

"You're right about that," agreed David. "You know, you might be smarter than you look."

Matt nudged David in the side, and nodded across the street. "Get this."

Walking out of The Purple Flamingo hair salon was a girl whose hair was dyed in strips of purple, red, orange, yellow, green and blue. It looked like a rainbow running down her head. Rainbow stripes also swirled across her long baggy sweat-shirt. Fluorescent green pants hugged her legs. On her feet she wore neon pink runners.

David shook his head while raspberry ribbon ice cream melted down his wrist.

The rainbow girl's friend had a single strip of black hair growing in long spikes up the middle of his shaved scalp. He wore neon pink runners, too, with blue jeans and a white T-shirt.

"Why do they do that?" muttered David.

Matt shook his head. "I heard that a pair of twins once came two hundred kilometres just to get their hair done at The Purple Flamingo."

"Freaky."

As the couple crossed the street, David read the words on Iroquois' T-shirt, "Have you hugged an Indian today?" Rain-bow had a grey cloud painted on her forehead. Brilliant blue raindrops rained down her cheeks.

"Freaky," repeated David.

"Awesome."

"Heavy."

"Maximum weird."

"Groovy."

"You're crazy," laughed Matt.

"You're crazy," echoed David. "Let's go find the next clue."

"Race you to the quarry."

Matt and David sped up Stony Road. Matt was in the lead as they skidded around the corner onto Bricker Street. A dump truck clunked up the road out of the quarry. The boys disappeared together into the hot cloud of dust.

When the dust had settled, Matt shaded his eyes against the bright sun and took a broad look around the hot quarry. Rocks were everywhere.

"There must be hundreds," said David.

"Thousands," whimpered Matt. Except

for a strip of sand down the middle of the quarry, there were rocks — jagged, smooth, large, small, scattered, heaped — everywhere.

"There's a million of them," Matt moaned. "We'll never find the next clue."

"Yes, we will," stated David calmly. "It will just take patience."

"Not for me," said Matt. He moved toward his bike.

"What do you mean?" yelled David.

"There's no way I'm spending all day down here turning over rocks," snarled Matt. He straightened his seat. "There might not even be another clue."

"Of course there is."

"Nobody's going to make a fool out of me over a fake treasure. I say forget it."

"Okay. Forget it," David shouted. He pulled up his socks and started throwing aside rocks. "But when I get through this and I've found the treasure, you can forget that, too."

"You won't find it," Matt stated, mounting his bike.

"Yes, I will," insisted David. "And if you quit now, it's all mine. And who will look like a fool then, Matt?"

The spinning wheels of Matt's bike kicked up a cloud of dust behind him. He looked back and saw David bending over, turning over rocks one by one.

Hot air brushed Matt's face as he pedalled through the grey dusty quarry toward the dirt road exit.

Who will look like a fool then?

At the side of the road was an old dump truck, barely yellow under a thick layer of dust. Its front tire was flat. Its windshield was broken.

Matt glanced back at David again. He was still bent over, throwing the rocks to one side. Matt knew he couldn't go back, but he couldn't just let David find the clue, either.

Matt veered quickly off the road behind the truck where there were, of course, more rocks. If he looked here, David wouldn't know he was looking. Maybe he could find the next clue and then the treasure, all on his own.

Matt leaned his bike against the side of the truck. In the dust on its door someone had drawn a big X. X marks the spot, thought Matt. Did this X?

Alongside the truck Matt began to tackle the rocks, the sun beating down hard as he worked. He pitched aside small rocks. The larger ones he rolled over. As he shoved and heaved, his hands became dusty and sore. The muscles in his back ached. Matt grunted as he straightened his sore back. Wiping the sweat from his brow left a streak of dirt across his red and shining face.

Peeking around the truck, Matt could see David very slowly now, turning over rocks. He was sure that X marked the spot where the next clue would be found, but he wished that the rock had been marked instead of just the truck. Licking his parched lips, Matt turned over more rocks and shoved them aside, hopeful each time of catching a glimpse of paper. He was bored with the scraping and clunking rocks. He could hear the distant rippling of the river. It sounded fresh and cool.

Matt heaved aside a large rock. At his feet lay an envelope. It took a moment for his heat-muddled mind to register its importance. He ran his sweating hands through his sandy hair and tucked the envelope into his pocket.

Matt got on his bike and rode straight to his secret spot on the other side of the river. There he splashed cool water over his face and tore the paper from the envelope.

6

Matt read the message on the dusty paper:

> Is a shop where they sell ham and
> Baloney
> What you want to know you will find
> Out
> And you could spend a pretty penny.
> The next clue is waiting for you
> There.

It didn't make any sense. It was so short. But "where they sell ham and baloney" could only mean one place.

Matt ambled into Joe's Deli on Stony Road. Joe stood behind the counter weighing a mound of sliced salami for Mrs. Miffin, while her two-year-old, Lisa, climbed out of her stroller. Matt glanced around quickly, trying to figure where the next clue would be planted.

He lifted the lid off the pickle barrel. The smell of garlic and vinegar rose from it, but there was nothing in the barrel but pickles. He put the cover back on.

Matt felt a tug on his shorts. "Hi, Lisa." He crouched down. "Lisa got a pickle?" Lisa nodded and stuck the pickle under Matt's nose. "No, thank you, Lisa," he said. "You eat it." Lisa stuck out her tongue and showed him the semi-chewed chunks of green. Matt groaned and looked away.

Under the edge of the counter, he saw lumps of old gum, but no paper. He eyed the boxes on the counter by the cash register, and around the cash register itself.

"Goodbye, Mrs. Miffin," Joe said. Then he turned to Matt, "You want something, young man?"

Matt pulled a hot pepperoni stick from the box on the counter and paid Joe for it. It wasn't a clue, but it was better than nothing.

Standing in front of the deli, biting the wrapper off his pepperoni, Matt looked up to see David sailing by on his BMX. David waved a slip of paper. "Another clue, Matt! Too bad for you!" David shot off up Stony Road.

Too bad for you, too, if your clue's as useless as mine, thought Matt. But why had he and David both found clues in the quarry? Matt looked again at the clue that had sent them there. "Under which *rocks* will *clues* be found?" it said.

Matt pedalled slowly up Stony Road. They probably needed both pieces of paper for the clue to make sense. If he could somehow get a look at David's note, maybe then he could figure out where to find the next clue. Matt chewed the spicy meat and followed David across the top of the north quarry wall.

When David parked his bike on the

bridge, so did Matt. Matt tried to look apologetic. "Sorry I got mad and didn't help you in the quarry," he said.

"I guess you are," scoffed David. "Especially since I found a clue."

"Yeah," said Matt. He hung his head, looking very sorry. "I just wish I had your..." He gulped. "...brains."

"Too bad for you," said David. He looked at the clue in his hand. Matt looked quickly and caught the words "Stony" and "care" before David snatched the paper away.

"Forget it," jeered David.

"David," said Matt, "didn't the note in the library say the *clues* in the quarry would be under *rocks*?"

"Yes. So what?"

"Did you find both clues?"

"Sure."

"So why aren't you over on Stony Road looking for the next clue?"

David pulled up his already pulled-up

socks and tucked in his already tucked-in shirt. "Maybe I've found the next clue already, too."

Matt pulled his part of the clue from his pocket and ran it slowly through his fingers in front of David's nose. "Oh, really?" he said.

"You sneak."

"Trouble is," said Matt, "your piece of the clue doesn't make much sense, does it?"

"How did you know?" David's fist was clenched tightly around his part of the clue.

" 'Cause mine doesn't either," admitted Matt.

"Let me see."

"Not till I see yours."

"We'll trade."

Slowly the boys exchanged slips of paper. Munching on the remains of his pepperoni, Matt read the note David had found:

> Out on the road that is called
> Stony
> That's not the one you care
> About,
> In a place where there are
> colours many
> Go to the part where you feel
> Hot air.

Matt stared at the paper and read it again. He was no farther ahead than before. Fritters. If David was smart enough to figure out his, he'd get the next clue by himself. David would get the treasure. He shouldn't have let David see...

"Even together," David was saying, "these notes don't make sense."

Matt reluctantly agreed. "It's just a jumble of words."

"Wait a minute," said David. "Read me your clue out loud."

Matt read.

"Okay, now listen." David read his slip of paper.

"So?"

"Words in yours rhyme with words in mine," David pointed out. "Baloney — Stony, out — about . . ."

"So what?"

"What if we put the two clues together, one line from mine, then one line from yours. Back and forth like that."

When the boys put their notes together the new clue read:

Out on the road that is called Stony
Is a shop where they sell ham and baloney.
That's not the one that you care about,
What you want to know you will find out
In a place where there are colours many
And you could spend a pretty penny.
Go to the part where you feed hot air.
The next clue is waiting for you there.

Matt burped a spicy burp. He grabbed David around the shoulders. "David, you're brilliant."

"Not brilliant enough to know where it means we should go."

"Think," said Matt. "Colours. You could spend a lot of money. Hot air. I know! The hair dryer at The Purple Flamingo!"

"Hey," laughed David, "you're really not as stupid as I thought."

"Gee, thanks. But there's still one problem. We can't just walk into The Purple Flamingo and check out the hair dryer."

"So, you go in and get your hair done and check the dryer then."

"No way." Matt shook his head. "*You* go in and get *your* hair done."

"Why me?"

"I figured out that's where the next clue is, so you can go in and get it."

"How much money do you have?" asked David.

"Not much. Why?"

"Even for something simple, The Purple Flamingo is pretty expensive. How about this? To get at the hair dryer, we'll use my money..."

"Yeah...?" Matt winced at what he knew was coming.

"And your head." David smiled. "Come on. I'll get my money."

Near the end of the path at the edge of the woods, David stopped suddenly. "Matt, look."

Matt looked across the Booth Street cul-de-sac. Standing on the sidewalk, talking together, were Matt's mother and Mr. Grubb.

"That guy gives me the creeps," said David.

"Me, too," agreed Matt. "There's always weird things in his garbage. Like one day there was a pair of lady's legs."

"I saw those, too," said David with a shudder.

"And what about all the strange boxes that get delivered there?"

"He buries people in his garden."

"What?"

"You know that book about the old

ladies who hire companions and then poison them and bury them in their garden?"

"No."

"I forgot," said David. "You wouldn't have read it."

"Well, what about it?"

"That's what Mr. Grubb does."

"How do you know?"

"I live right next door to him, remember?"

"Cree-eepy," commented Matt.

"You're not kidding. The smells sometimes that come out of there..."

Matt grimaced. Just then Mr. Grubb turned his sagging face in their direction. The spikes of hair in his bushy eyebrows jerked up and down, and his eyes opened wide.

David turned and pedalled furiously into the wooded ravine. Matt followed.

7

Waiting for The Purple Flamingo to open, David patted Matt's sandy-brown mop of curls. "May I suggest," he teased, "the Halo of Many Coloured Spikes? Or perhaps the Pink Pouff would suit you rather well."

Behind them the door clicked unlocked. Matt stood to go in.

"Good luck," David said.

When Matt stepped into The Purple Flamingo, strange smells tickled his nostrils. The shop owner, with rainbow hair and clouds and raindrops on her face, filed her blue fingernails. Looking at the list of hairstyles and prices on the board, Matt decided she must have the Summer Storm.

"What do you want?" Summer Storm

shouted above the din of the music blasting from the radio.

For the amount David had given him to spend, Matt could choose between The Bald Eagle and The Purple Flamingo.

"What's a Bald Eagle?" asked Matt.

The woman stood and wrapped her fingers around Matt's head just above his ears. "Everything from here up we shave off. Then we rub in something to keep your hair from growing too fast and bake it under the dryer. You know, so you can keep The Bald Eagle look for a while."

Matt gulped. "What about The Purple Flamingo?"

"We bring a thin piece of hair down each side of your head and set it with a gel to form the flamingo's legs. On top we shape a flamingo's head and set it with gel, too. Your hair is curly so we could skip the rollers and just fluff up the rest. Then we spray the whole thing with purple talcum powder."

"Would I go under the hair dryer for that one?" asked Matt.

"On the no-blow setting. You know, to help set the shape of the head and legs."

Matt swallowed. "Okay."

"You sure? Some people don't like The Purple Flamingo much because it only lasts till the next time you wash your hair."

"That's ... okay."

"Okay. You need your hair washed first. Go to the back of the shop and behind that wall to the left." Summer Storm returned her attention to her blue nails.

Matt walked stiffly to the back of the store. The person beside the sink smiled a green smile. "You're that cute little friend of Martha's, aren't you?" the husky voice gushed. "My name is Ecstacy. Oh, I can't wait to run my hands through those beautiful curls."

Matt mustered all his courage not to

turn and run. He slumped into the chair. Ecstacy tied a plastic apron around him and lowered his head back into the stream of warm water. "If it gets too hot," she drawled, "let me know."

Ecstacy massaged shampoo through Matt's hair. Her long nails stabbed and jabbed his scalp. The hard edge of the basin dug into the back of his neck.

Ecstacy moaned along with the blaring music as she rinsed the shampoo from Matt's hair. Suddenly the water went icy cold. Matt sprang upright, spraying Ecstacy and dripping icy water into the back of his shirt.

"That's good for your scalp," drawled Ecstacy. "Don't you like it?"

Matt shook his head and shuddered. Ecstacy tipped him back again and squeezed the water from his hair. It felt as if she was wringing his hair right out of his head. Then she threw a bright yellow towel over Matt's head and rubbed vigorously. His scalp tingled.

"Done," she finally declared. Matt glanced in the mirror to see if he still had hair.

Summer Storm yanked the comb through Matt's wet curls. He winced with each snag and tangle. David stood outside with his nose to the window. Matt smiled at him faintly.

"That your friend?"

"Sort of."

"Is he going to get done, too?"

"No."

"Too bad. With that straight black hair, we could do him a great Iroquois."

"Yeah. Too bad."

Finally Summer Storm set down the comb. Matt sucked in his breath when a cold glop of goo plopped on the top of his head. A flamingo's head began to take shape, and Matt began to wish he and David had never put their two clues together. Summer Storm fluffed the purple "feathers" all around his head. "Just a little trim and you're ready for the dryer."

As the cold razor buzzed and nipped at the back of his neck, Matt looked in the mirror at the stupid-looking kid with the stupid-looking purple flamingo sitting on his head. He wished it wasn't him.

Matt stood to go to the dryer. David

held up the scraps of paper. Matt shot him a scathing look. Did David really think he had forgotten why he was here? Did he think he was having a good time?

Matt gave the outside of the hair dryer a quick inspection. No clue was attached to the surface. That's okay, Matt told himself as he sat down. It's probably inside the dome.

Summer Storm flipped a couple of switches and lowered the dome over his head. Matt felt like part of a science-fiction movie. He raised his eyes to check the inside rim. There was nothing there. He checked the floor around the chair in case the clue had fallen or blown out. Nothing. He lifted the dryer off his head so he could check further up inside it.

"What's the matter?" asked Summer Storm. "Is it too hot?"

"No," said Matt. "I mean ... uh ... yes. Sort of." He uttered a feeble laugh.

Summer Storm turned down the heat. Matt squirmed in the chair, feeling around for a slip of paper, but all he felt was the smooth vinyl seat. He ran his hands frantically over the warm surfaces of the dryer.

"You have to sit still or your Flamingo won't set," warned Summer Storm.

Matt shoved the dryer off. "I've got to go." He tore off his plastic apron.

"But your Flamingo..."

Matt threw his money on the desk and slammed the door behind him.

David pointed to Matt's head and laughed. "Who's your friend?"

"It's a Purple Flamingo," answered Matt in disgust.

"You look terrible," said David, "but at least we can get on with the treasure hunt now."

"Wrong," said Matt.

"What?"

"There was no clue."

"What??" David repeated.

"I said there was no clue."

"Did you check...?"

"I checked everything," shouted Matt. "Over and over. You think I wanted to look like this for nothing?"

"I'm sorry. I shouldn't have let you do this."

"There's nothing to be sorry about. You said a long time ago this whole thing was fishy. You were right. We should never have even looked for the next clue." Matt yanked the crumpled remains of the other notes out of his pockets and tossed them in the basket. "The treasure hunt is over. If we weren't so stupid, it would never have gone this far." He shoved his hands deep in his pockets and headed across the street.

David followed. "Where are you going?"

"To get rid of this," yelled Matt, tugging at his purple hair. "Where do you think?"

8

Matt stormed into the ice cream store. He almost collided with a couple coming out hand in hand. Her strawberry-pink ice cream matched her hair. His pistachio-green matched his.

Matt charged through the door to the washroom in the back of the store. He shoved his head under the tap, muttering crossly. David sat in silence on the floor. The sink filled with purple water.

"You know what, Matt?"

"Can't hear you," snapped Matt from under the tap.

Looking up at Matt, David noticed something on the underside of the hand dryer. It was a piece of paper. Carefully he removed it and unfolded it. Right away he recognized the tight, squeezed-up printing.

"Matt," shouted David. "Look what I found." He turned off the taps.

Matt looked. "Where?"

"On the bottom of the hand dryer."

"Where you feel hot air." Matt recalled the words in the last note. "We were supposed to be looking here? Not in The Purple Flamingo?"

"But what about the 'colours many'?" said David, looking around at the grey walls.

"How many flavours of ice cream do they sell here?" Matt said.

"Of course," groaned David. "I guess the treasure hunt is still on, eh?"

Matt shook the water from his once-again brown hair. "I don't know. Let's see the note. I'm not doing anything stupid like that again."

David flattened the paper against the wall. It said:

You've come a long way.
You're almost through.
There's not much more you have
To do
There's a house on Booth much
Bigger than the rest.
In the corner of its yard, an
Old bird's nest.
Don't worry about disturbing
The birds.
There aren't any in there,
Only words.

"Isn't that...?" Matt asked weakly.

David nodded. "Mr. Grubb's."

"Frittering fudgsicles," cursed Matt. "Haven't we done enough?" Then he grabbed a wad of paper towels and squeezed the water from his hair.

Moments later the boys were staring at the only house on Booth that was "much bigger than the rest." It was a huge, dark two-storey house. Some of its bricks were broken, and the paint around the eaves and top-floor windows was cracked and peeling. Around it grew a tall, prickly hedge. It was the biggest house on the biggest lot on the street.

David nodded. "So the next clue is in Mr. Grubb's yard."

Suddenly one of the dirty windows of the big house sprang open. Clouds of smoke billowed from the window — green smoke that seemed to crawl over the windowsill and slither to the floor of the porch. Then the grey form of Mr. Grubb appeared at the window. He slammed the window shut.

Without taking his eyes from the window, Matt whispered, "Did you see...?"

David just whimpered in reply.

Then the boys raced around the corner and hid behind the hedge. Matt peeked through the quivering leaves, sure that the sound of his thudding heart would give him away. The front door opened and the old man appeared, carry-

ing a bag bulging with.... Matt didn't
want to guess.

The shrill squeak of the gate opening
broke the deadly quiet of the hot morn-
ing. Again, when Mr. Grubb pulled the
gate shut behind him, what sounded like a
scream of pain sprang from its hinges.

Then the large grey owner of the
large strange house shuffled down Booth

Street and disappeared into the ravine.

"I don't like the look of this at all," said Matt.

"Are you scared?" asked David.

"Are you?"

David nodded. "But I'm curious."

Matt shuddered. "Well, don't forget," he warned. "Curiosity killed the dog."

"Curiosity killed the cat," corrected David.

"Whatever."

The boys crept around the outside edges of Mr. Grubb's yard. Thick bramble bushes pushed against a dilapidated wooden fence at the back of the property. Growing in the back corner of the yard, just beyond the brambles, was an oddly shaped tree with one dead branch. On it sat the scraggly remains of a bird nest.

"That's it," said Matt.

David nodded solemnly. "The note in that nest could take us to the treasure."

Matt thought about the note in the nest through a quiet lunch. Leaving most of his sandwich on the plate, he mumbled excuses to his mother.

He pedalled alone into the ravine to his quiet spot by the river. Bump, rattle rattle, dip down, dip up, sharp turn right, narrow narrow, boulder, through the bushes, and down the bank.

Matt flipped a stone into the water. It did not skip, but sank immediately to the bottom of the river.

The treasure hunt was over. He knew exactly where the next clue was. But he also knew that he and David could not go into Mr. Grubb's yard to get it.

Matt flung another stone across the water. Three skips. There had to be another way of getting the clue.

What if they climbed up on the wall between David's yard and Mr. Grubb's? Matt thought the nest looked too far over, but maybe it wasn't.

Or, if it was too far, they could use

a ladder, and one of them could crawl along the branch. It would have to be David. He was lighter. Besides, Matt had done one scary thing. David could do this one. But what if the branch wouldn't take even David's weight? David would go crashing into the brambles and be trapped in Mr. Grubb's yard.

If only there was a way of getting into the yard knowing for sure that Mr. Grubb wouldn't see them. Like, if they knew Mr. Grubb was asleep...

That was it! He knew how they could get the note in the tree. He flipped a flat stone at the creek and counted. Fourteen skips. Ha! They would find this treasure yet!

Matt scrambled up the bank and through the bushes to the boulder. He couldn't wait to tell David he'd figured out how to get at the nest!

Matt leaned his bike against David's house, beside the red BMX, and ran into his backyard. He expected to find David reading in the hammock, but the hammock hung emptily between the trees. Matt was about to leave. Then he spotted him.

David was kneeling on the top of the stone wall near the back corner of his yard. Matt stepped nearer. He saw David reaching for the abandoned nest on the dead branch of the tree in Mr. Grubb's yard.

David was trying to get the next clue! Without him!

9

"Hey!"

When Matt shouted, David lost his balance. He almost toppled into the yard next door, but at the last moment, he threw himself into his own.

"What's the big idea?" yelled Matt.

"What do you mean?" Blushing, David wiped the sweat from his brow.

"Going ahead on the treasure hunt, without me," accused Matt. "What do you think?"

"I thought if we could get the next clue without going right into his yard..."

"*We* were not going for the next clue. *You* were. Alone."

David shrugged.

"You were going to try for the trea-

sure without me, weren't you? My
treasure!"

"*Your* treasure?" David folded his
arms. "You never would have got this far
without me, and you know it."

"Would, too!"

"No, you wouldn't! You're a quitter.
Every time the treasure hunt got a little
bit tough, you quit! I should never have
agreed to split the treasure with you."

Fists clenched on his hips, Matt stepped closer to David. "It was never yours to split." He thrust his face forward. "*I'm* the one who got the postcard, remember?"

"Sure, I remember who got the postcard. I also remember who helped you with the clue in the library and who found the clue under the hand dryer."

"You didn't even know the clue was there! If I hadn't had the guts to go into The Purple Flamingo, you never would have been near the hand dryer in the ice cream store."

David laughed. "Oh, you had the guts, all right." He grabbed his book out of the hammock and marched out of his yard. "And the stupidity."

Matt followed.

David mounted his glistening red BMX. Pedalling toward the ravine path, he shouted, "What a stupid waste of *my* money that was!"

Matt stormed after him, cursing his

dangling bike chain that again needed adjusting. He spurted to catch up. Pulling alongside David, he said, "Maybe I'm not as smart as you, but at least I'm not a traitor."

"I am not a traitor," snarled David.

"Then what were you doing on the wall without me?"

"The nest was still out of reach."

"But what if you could have reached it?" pressed Matt. "You were going to cut me out, weren't you?"

"If you think I'm a traitor," David sneered, "then I guess you have your answer."

Matt pulled ahead and turned suddenly into David's path. David swerved to avoid colliding with him. His front wheel caught the edge of the pavement. The gleaming red bicycle crashed to the ground, pinning David underneath it. Matt continued into the ravine.

"I can't move," David groaned.

Matt turned. "So what? You've got a

book in your pocket. Why don't you read it?" He left David lying on the path.

Tears stung in Matt's eyes, but he moved on. Soon he was nestled in the sand by his spot on the river.

Matt hadn't wanted to involve David in the adventure to start with. Why had he started to trust him? What if he hadn't caught him up on the wall? What if David had reached the nest? Would he have told Matt he had the next clue? Matt sighed. Why did he want so much to believe that David had not intended to cut him out of the adventure?

David had called him a quitter, and stupid. But Matt knew he was no brain. And he *had* wanted to give up, more than once.

Matt thought about all the riding they had done together since that first day on the bridge, about sharing ice cream cones, about their adventures tracking down clues.

Then he knew why it mattered if David was planning to go ahead without him. You can only be a traitor to a friend. And that's what David had become, sometime when Matt wasn't looking.

Matt went back to where he had left David, but David was gone. He rode back past David's house, but his bike was not there. He continued on, around the corner past Mr. Grubb's yard, through the schoolyard, and on down Stony Road, but there was no sign of David or his bike anywhere.

Matt ambled into the variety store and slumped on the counter. Martha pushed back a wisp of hair and slid her glasses up her nose. "Why so sad?" she asked. "It can't be that bad."

"Martha, have you ever done anything really rotten to anybody?"

"I made Lisa eat her vegetables once when I was babysitting her. Rotten like that?"

"No. I mean like to a friend."

"I told Ecstacy she was ugly once."

"She is."

"But it was still rotten for me to say so. It really hurt her feelings."

"What did she do?"

"She said I was plain and that I was jealous of how she looked because I didn't have enough money to spend on makeup and getting my hair done and all that."

"Did you get mad?"

"At first. Then I realized I am plain, and that people sometimes say things they know will hurt you when they're feeling hurt or insecure somehow."

"So, what did you do?"

"I apologized."

"Even though she is ugly?"

"Ecstacy's not really ugly once you get to know her."

Matt moved back thoughtfully from the counter. "I guess lots of people aren't what you think at first."

The bell on the door of the store jingled. Matt looked up. He almost hoped it would be Ecstacy, so he could look at her and try to see her as not ugly.

"Now remember, Lisa," Matt heard Mrs. Miffin say, "just look. Don't touch."

"Yook don't touch," shouted Lisa, running up and down the aisles. "Yook don't touch!" She ran up to Matt and wrapped her pudgy arms around his legs, until Matt managed to escape.

Matt rode and rode. Finally he found David at the wooden bridge, dangling his feet in the water, reading his book. Matt had looked and looked for David, but now that he had found him, his stomach went into knots.

Matt lay down his bike and said, "I'm sorry, David. Were you hurt?"

David continued to read.

"David?"

"It depends what you mean. If you're talking about my scraped leg, not really. If you're talking about being called a traitor..."

"I'm sorry. The way it looked..."

"You accused me of something before

you even knew the facts. Where were you after lunch?"

Matt tried to remember. David went on. "Your mom said you'd gone riding, but I couldn't find you." Matt remembered where he had been. No one would find him there.

David continued. "So I thought I'd at least see if my idea for getting the nest was possible. I figured you'd show up eventually." David set his book down between them. "And you did, but before I could explain, you started in about *your* treasure, and the next thing I know I'm lying under my bike and you're riding away."

Matt stared at the sunlight glinting on the ripples of water below them. Then he said, "You know how you're smarter than me?"

David sighed.

"Well, you are."

"So?"

"Well, after lunch I thought of a way

for us to get the clue in the nest, and it wouldn't be dangerous, well, hardly at all. So I came racing over to tell you about it. I felt good, because I knew you had kind of kept us going up till now. I thought if I figured out about the clue in the nest..."

David nodded. "So you come into my yard. It looks like I'm about to get the clue without you. So much for your chance to show off your brainy idea."

"Yeah."

"So you decide I'm a traitor and who knows what else and cut me off in the path."

"You were really bugging me, David. Just like when school's on. Acting so superior."

David nodded. "When you started in about *your* treasure, I thought you were going to cut me out of the hunt."

"I thought *you* were trying to cut *me* out," said Matt. The boys were silent for a moment.

"So what was your idea?" asked David, pulling his feet from the water. "About the clue in the nest?"

"Do you have a tent?"

"No."

"That's okay. I do."

"What does a tent have to do with the note in the nest?"

"Would your parents let us sleep out in your backyard tonight?" asked Matt. "In my tent?"

"Probably. But..."

"Out in the tent we wait. And when everyone is asleep, under cover of darkness..."

David nodded and smiled.

10

Out in Matt's nylon tent, the boys waited. The last sliver of orange sun disappeared behind the school. Blackness closed in on the neighbourhood.

No light shone from the dark bulk of the house next door. The blinds on its upstairs windows were down. Behind one of them, guessed the boys, slept Mr. Grubb. Behind the other? They hated to imagine.

Without a word, the boys left the tent. On silent feet they stole out of the yard and down David's driveway. At the sidewalk, Matt stopped suddenly. David bumped into him.

"Sshh!" warned Matt. But the only sound was the crickets chirping in the long grass by the creek. Moths fluttered silently around the streetlights. A cat on the Lennoxes' porch watched as the two boys in pyjamas crept along the hedge in front of the dark Grubb house.

Matt stopped at the gate and took the lid off the bottle of cooking oil he carried. He dribbled oil down each of the rusty hinges. Then he set the bottle down and lifted the catch on the gate. He pushed. Slowly. All quiet, he made the okay sign with his fingers.

The boys stepped beyond the silent gate. In one of the front windows, the window of the green smoke, a strange play of light and dark froze Matt in mid-step. Had something inside the house moved? Or was it just the flickering reflection of a streetlight? And what was that rustling in the bushes by the rickety porch? David grabbed the sleeve of Matt's pyjamas. Matt gasped.

Together the boys followed their eerie shadows into the dreaded yard. Creeping through the damp, overgrown grass, Matt tried hard not to imagine creatures in the ivy that clung to the walls of the house.

"How did you talk me into this?" whispered David.

Matt glanced at the back of the old house, still in darkness, blinds still down. He continued on tiptoe toward the crooked tree.

"Do you think we'll be able to reach the nest?" Matt whispered. "It looks pretty high. David?" Matt turned. "David?"

But David was gone.

Matt scanned the yard frantically for his partner. Beside a gnarled rose bush stood a shovel. What had David told him about bodies in the garden? Matt strained his eyes in the darkness. Nowhere among the trees and bushes could he see David. Matt gulped. Should he stay here, where the trees seemed to be coming to life around him? Or escape while he had the chance? Where was David? Had he chickened out and gone back to his yard? Or had he been mysteriously taken into . . . that house? Matt shuddered.

Then, he saw him.

"What . . .?" Matt ran to where David stood by the back door. David was poking through a stack of paperback books on a TV tray.

"Frittering fudgsicles! This is not a friendly trip to the library —!"

Suddenly, from inside the house came a *zzzt-zzzzt* sound and a brilliant flash of blue. There was the sound of water sloshing. David dropped the book. Matt hunched against the wall and listened. Slowly he stood, peering over the windowsill into the kitchen.

An old-fashioned camera on a very tall tripod stood in the middle of the room. A large clock was attached to the tripod. Tubes ran from the sink to various pots around the room. More tubes ran out of the room to other parts of the house. The taps were running water through some of the tubes and into the sink. When the water reached the top of the sink, the taps shut off. But there was no one there.

Matt and David looked at each other, wide-eyed. Again they heard the *zzzt-zzzzt*, followed by the brilliant blue flash. Matt pulled David away from the window.

"This house is haunted," he whispered. "Come on. The clue. Before it's too late."

The boys crossed the long yard. Cold water squooshed between their toes. The chill breeze made them shiver in their light pyjamas. From the corner of the yard, the twisted branches of the tree seemed to beckon them closer, daring them to try and get the note from the nest.

Matt looked at David. "Just a tree, right?"

"Right." Matt hunched over beside the tree. David climbed on Matt's back.

"Ooogh!" complained Matt. "Your feet are wet!" He wobbled under David's weight. David snatched at the clump of

dried twigs on the branch. Together they fell in a heap — Matt David, and the abandoned bird nest.

Matt moaned. "You're heavy — He clutched David arm and squeezed. "Look."

The blind on upper window was up. Behind the smeary glass was the grey shape of a very large man. The grey shape turned, leaving the window empty.

"He's coming," wailed David.

Matt grabbed the nest and scrambled to his feet. "We've got to get out of here before he gets downstairs."

Matt and David scurried toward the gate, tripping over their own and each other's feet. They were almost there when they heard the deep, bellowing laughter of a maniac ghost.

Huffing and panting, they ran until they were safely back inside the tent. They snuggled, shivering, deep into their sleeping bags.

Matt shone a flashlight onto the note in David's shaking hands. "Hold it still," he giggled.

David used both hands to steady the paper. "But you're the one who's shaking."

He took a deep breath and read:

You've come very close to my big
House old,
But to come right inside, are you
That bold?
To get at the treasure, thats what
You must do,
So into my home I'm inviting you.
Go down the hall, take the second
Right,

And in that room you will see the
Sight
For which you've been searching
All this time.
But I warn you now- there's
Another rhyme.

"Mr. Grubb wrote these notes?"
wailed Matt.

"Looks like it," said David.

Matt pulled his sleeping bag over his
head. David reread the words of the note
and clicked off the flashlight.

"Mr. Grubb!" said David. "I was sure
it was Martha."

"You were wrong, for once." Matt
poked his head back out of his sleeping
bag. "I was kind of hoping a stranger did
it. Like, you know that show where the
guy goes around mysteriously sending people a million dollars? Somebody like that."

"Maybe Mr. Grubb is somebody like
that," considered David.

"I doubt it," muttered Matt.

David lay with his arms folded behind his head, staring up at the darkness. "It was pretty clever of the old creep just the same."

"Mmm," murmured Matt.

"I wonder what the treasure is?"

"Who cares? We're not going into that house just because some note says to. Especially after what we saw tonight."

David said nothing.

"Right, David?" Matt said firmly.

"We've been over there once already," argued David. "At night. What could be scarier than that?"

"There's a big difference between sneaking around somebody's yard when they're sleeping, and going right into their house."

"I've got to know why Mr. Grubb did this," said David. "I'm going in whether you do or not. You quit if you want. I don't care."

Matt stared up at the ceiling of the tent and sighed.

Wishing he had never seen the mysterious postcard, he rolled over and pulled his sleeping bag over his head.

11

Pretending to read comics on Matt's front porch, Matt and David waited and watched, and watched and waited.

Finally Mr. Grubb emerged from the big old house at the end of the street. Slowly he shuffled down the steps, down the walk, and opened the gate. He paused. He closed the gate and stuck a finger in one ear, then the other. A puzzled look crossed his sour face. Then he bent down to look at the bottle of cooking oil beside the hedge. He shook his head and coughed. It sounded almost like a laugh.

On a sheet of paper Matt scribbled the message: *Dear Mom — Gone to Mr. Grubb's with David.*

David was right. They couldn't back

out now. Not after coming this close. Besides, if David could do this, so could he.

Again only the Lennoxes' cat watched as the boys approached the house. No smoke billowed from its windows. There were no flashes of light. The only sound was the creaking of the old wooden stairs.

Matt took a deep breath. Together the boys opened the front door and stepped into the house. The screen door sprang shut behind them.

In the musty-smelling hall, pictures of Mr. Grubb and what must be his ancestors lined the walls. The eyes in the photos followed the boys as they tiptoed past. Big dark shapes in the room on the left seemed to be waiting for them.

"It's just furniture," David whispered.

"Sure," squeaked Matt. "What else?"

Through the silent dingy hall they crept.

"The second door," whispered Matt.

David nodded. The boys exchanged brave smiles. They turned the corner into the room.

And there it was. The "treasure." Something old with something new. Big parts and little parts. Okay for one, but better for two. And different. No one could have guessed it, but it made perfect sense.

"A computer!" Matt raved. Forgetting to be afraid, he dashed across the room to Mr. Grubb's antique rolltop desk. "How did Mr. Grubb know I wanted a computer? Now I can play anytime I want. No more fighting for space at the video game at the ice cream store. No more bugging my parents for one when I know they'll say no. This is great!"

"Sure," said David. "If you're keen on playing video games with the Boogy Man of Booth Street."

Matt's voice was suddenly very quiet. "What?"

"Listen." David read the note that had been taped to the front of the monitor.

The end of a treasure hunt calls
For celebration,
So now's the time to offer you a
Special invitation
To play computer games with me
And Betsy any day
That you have asked your mothers
And they've said it's okay.
I knew you'd come here first
With me gone somehow,
But into the computer, LOAD
"TREASURE HUNT," now.

"That's no treasure," complained Matt. "And who's Betsy? The Wicked Witch of the West?"

"Yeah, probably."

"Fritters," mumbled Matt. "Let's go."

"Wait a sec. What are all these pipes and tubes and wires and things? They're all hooked up to the computer." David

and Matt studied the wires spilling from the back of the computer.

"It's probably a trap," insisted Matt. "Let's go."

A twisting mess of red and yellow wires trailed out of the room. David followed it into the hall, around the corner, and deeper into the house. Soon Matt found himself standing in the kitchen, where red wires snaked across the floor to the sink. There they joined to an octopus-like contraption with green tubes stretching around the room to various exotic plants.

Zz-zzzt! Before Matt could remember why that sound was familiar, a flash of blue light filled the kitchen. Matt turned. The yellow wire wiggled across the floor to the tripod. A photograph of one of the strange plants with the time printed in the bottom corner slid from the camera into a tray. The camera rotated on the top of the tripod. When the second hand on the large clock reached the twelve, there was another *zz-zzzt*, another flash of blue and, moments later, another photo slid into the tray.

"That weirdo has programmed his computer to water his plants and take pictures of them?" exclaimed Matt. "I don't believe it."

"Weird." David shook his head in amazement.

The boys stepped carefully over the cords and followed another set of wires until it came to a closed door.

"We'd better not open it," said Matt. He glanced uneasily over his shoulder at the empty furniture in the room behind them.

David put his hand on the knob. "Why not?"

"Well...we weren't invited in there."

"Yeah," agreed David. "It's probably locked anyway." He turned the knob. The door opened.

"Phew. That smell." Matt covered his nose. "It's like the stuff they used at The Purple Flamingo. Only stronger."

Inside the room all kinds of glass bottles and beakers and metal pots and tubing perched and twisted on tables. In some of the containers brilliantly coloured liquids glistened and shone.

"What does he *do* in here?"

"Remember the green smoke?" asked Matt.

"How could I forget?" croaked David. A single bubble burbled through a beaker of red liquid and popped. David pulled the door shut quickly.

More wires of various colours and thicknesses spread along the hallway and up the shadowy staircase.

"No way," insisted Matt, before David could even suggest going up.

"Then let's go load in 'TREASURE HUNT' now," argued David. "Just to see what happens." Matt wanted to leave. But again he found himself following David. David typed in the LOAD "TREASURE HUNT" command. The light flashed on the whirring disk drive. While the screen flashed brilliant colours faster than you could see, popping noises came from the next room and water started running in the kitchen.

"That's enough." Matt turned to go. Then the computer began to sing:

I am Betsy and I know some games that you know,
Like Bookworm and Baseball, and so many more...

"Ecstacy!" shouted Matt. "That's Ecstacy's voice!"

"Sshh! Listen!"

"What's she...?"

But the best things are for the Computer Club,
That you can join...with Mr. Archibald Grubb.

"Those two weirdos...?" puzzled Matt.

David shuddered. "I think we better get out of here," he stammered, "while we still can."

"Finally we agree. Let's go!"

But in the doorway they were stopped cold by the towering bulk of Mr. Archibald Grubb.

12

The old man's deep, gravelly voice rumbled, "I declare this the first official meeting of the computer club..."

Matt felt faint. Images of the old man, the computer, wires and tubes twisting and turning, spun around and around in his head. Suddenly the metallic voice of the computer began again. *"I am Betsy and I know some..."* Mr. Grubb reached out his long arm and the voice was silenced.

"....of David, Matt, and Archibald Grubb," he mumbled quietly. "That's me."

Matt felt himself nodding. David was nodding, too.

"Sit down, Matt," growled the grey voice. "You're the baseball star, aren't you?" Mr. Grubb stabbed at the keyboard with his long bony fingers.

Matt sat. David moved backwards toward the door. "You sit, too," ordered Mr. Grubb. David sat.

Tiny red and blue players scrambled around the computer screen. Thinking only of escape, Matt mechanically controlled the joystick for the blue players.

The red pitcher threw a fast ball. The blue batter hit it, and the ball sailed high over the fence. "Home run!" shouted the machine-like voice of the umpire. Matt's blue player sauntered easily around the bases. Matt almost laughed.

Then he realized he had almost let the baseball game fool him into feeling safe. He shook his head. "I've got to go," he said. "My..." But before he could finish, his player's foot touched home plate and a small drawer shot out from under the computer. It was full of jujubes. With his mouth hanging open, Matt looked from the jujubes to the old man and back to the jujubes.

Mr. Grubb threw back his head. Deep, bellowing laughter filled the room. Matt looked at the huge shaking man beside him, too large for his frayed grey clothes. Mr. Grubb laughed and laughed, and his jowly face grew redder and redder.

Matt glanced at David and nodded at the door. But as the boys started to ease themselves out of their seats, Mr. Grubb stopped laughing as suddenly as he had begun. He wiped tears from the wrinkled corners of his eyes. "I can't remember the last time I laughed like that," he said. "Thank you, Matt."

Matt shrugged.

"Now," growled Mr. Grubb. "Who likes lemonade?"

"I do," answered David.

Matt shot David an angry look.

"Good," boomed Mr. Grubb. "I'll make some." He lifted his big body from the chair. Then he shuffled into the big kitchen at the back of the house.

"What's with '*I do*'?" snapped Matt, as soon as Mr. Grubb had left the room. "We've got to get out of here."

"Come on, Matt. It would be rude to leave when he's getting us a drink."

"You're worried about being rude? He could be mixing up a batch of poison."

"You boys coming?" Mr. Grubb called from the kitchen.

"See?" said David. "He's harmless."

Matt followed David reluctantly into the kitchen. The camera and tripod were leaning against the corner now. Mr. Grubb was impatiently yanking plastic tubing out of the sink and trying to cram it into a cupboard. He mumbled, "Never works. Stupid thing. Sit down."

Matt rolled his eyes at David.

"Now, what...?" Mr. Grubb closed his eyes and held his head in his hands. "Lemonade!" he exclaimed. "Lemons!" He gathered lemons from the refrigerator and set them on the table.

Matt and David watched as the old man cut the lemons in half. His huge hands squeezed the juice into a glass pitcher.

"Doesn't Betsy help you make the lemonade?" asked David.

"Ho, ho, oh, no," growled Mr. Grubb. "Some things must be done...the natural way. I have tried to get Betsy to make lemonade...hooked her up to a Cuisinart, but the pair of them..." He chuckled. "I just couldn't get them to quit blowing fuses."

Mr. Grubb spooned golden honey from a clay pot into the lemonade.

"Yup, some things are best left to old-fashioned ways." He waved an arm in the direction of the computer room. "This new-fangled technology is okay for some things, but..." With a long wooden spoon he stirred the lemonade. Ice cubes clinked against the glass.

"But why make lemonade the hard

way?" remarked Matt. "My mom just opens a package and dumps it in a glass of water."

"Taste." Mr. Grubb held out the spoon to Matt.

Matt slurped the icy liquid from the spoon. "Mmm," he exclaimed.

"Ever taste lemonade like that before?"

Matt licked his lips and shook his head. "Mmmmm."

"Here, David, you taste."

"Mmmm," David agreed.

Mr. Grubb poured the icy drink into three glasses. "Dumps a package in a glass of water and calls it lemonade. Tsk, tsk. I bet you pull a Captain Seafood package out of the freezer and call it fish, too."

Matt shrugged and nodded.

"You know, when I was a boy we used to catch fish right out of Pebble Creek and cook 'em up for supper."

Matt and David sipped their lemonade while Mr. Grubb talked on.

"I remember one place I loved to fish. It was beautiful there, the way the sandy bank just sort of curved around. I'd just lean back in it with my line dangling in the water, and look up in the trees. It was kind of a tricky place to get at, so nobody knew about it but me. Other kids came along the path sometimes, but they always turned around when they came to this boulder. Looked like a dead end. I wonder if that old boulder's still there..."

"It is," Matt broke in. He could hardly believe it. *His* secret place had been Mr. Grubb's secret place, all those years ago. "I found that spot, too. It's been my own secret place for a long time." Matt looked at the old man's face again. There was a sparkle in his grey eyes, and suddenly, behind the bushy eyebrows and saggy cheeks, Matt saw the face of a young boy. "At least, I thought it was."

Matt looked over at David. Until now, he hadn't thought of sharing his special spot with anyone. It seemed to be a place for him alone. But maybe it was a place to share, too, with a friend.

Matt suddenly stood up and gulped down the rest of his lemonade. "Come on, David. You've got to see this place."

David jumped up eagerly and started to follow Matt out of the room. At the doorway, the two boys stopped and looked behind them. Mr. Grubb was busily clearing up the lemonade glasses.

Matt looked at David. Then he walked back over to the old man and held out his hand. "Thanks a lot, Mr. Grubb. We'll be back tomorrow, okay?"

Mr. Grubb solemnly shook Matt's hand. "I'd like that, my friend," he said, smiling. "I'd like that very much."

About the Author

Kathy Stinson has published five picture books including *RED IS BEST, MOM AND DAD DON'T LIVE TOGETHER ANY MORE* and *THE BARE NAKED BOOK.* Her first book, *RED IS BEST,* won the 1982 IODE Award and several of her stories have been published in other countries such as France, Great Britain, Sweden, and Venezuela.

Before she became a writer, Kathy did many different kinds of jobs. She sorted mail, taught school, waited on tables, mothered two children and ran programs for pre-schoolers. She now lives in Toronto where she writes picture books for little children and longer stories for older readers. She also travels across Canada talking to children about her books and her writing career and, in 1987 she took part in the first exchange of children's authors between Canada and England.